PASTURE TO MARKET

NATURE'S MAKERS

JULIE KNUTSON

Published in the United States of America by Cherry Lake Publishing
Ann Arbor, Michigan
www.cherrylakepublishing.com

Content Advisors: Gretta Winkelbauer, owner, Gretta's Goats

Photo Credits: © Paulina Coletta, cover, 1, 8; © Courtney Oertel, 5, 12, 14,17, 18,20, 24; © Tyler Rudick, 6; © Gretta Winkelbauer, 11; © JASPERIMAGE/Shutterstock.com, 13; © Hethers/Shutterstock.com, 23; © Paul Natkin, 26; © Val Thoermer/Shutterstock.com, 28

Library of Congress Cataloging-in-Publication Data
Names: Knutson, Julie, author. | Knutson, Julie. Nature's makers.
Title: Pasture to market / by Julie Knutson.
Description: Ann Arbor : Cherry Lake Publishing, 2019. | Series: Nature's makers | Includes bibliographical references and index.
Identifiers: LCCN 2018036615| ISBN 9781534143029 (hardcover) | ISBN 9781534140783 (pdf) | ISBN 9781534139589 (pbk.) | ISBN 9781534141988 (hosted ebook)
Subjects: LCSH: Goat farming—Juvenile literature. | Goat industry—Juvenile literature. | Farms, Small—Juvenile literature.
Classification: LCC SF383.35 .K58 2019 | DDC 636.3/91—dc23
LC record available at https://lccn.loc.gov/2018036615

Cherry Lake Publishing would like to acknowledge the work of The Partnership for 21st Century Learning. Please visit www.p21.org for more information.

Printed in the United States of America
Corporate Graphics

ABOUT THE AUTHOR

Julie Knutson is a former teacher who writes from her home in northern Illinois. Researching these books involved sampling a range of farm products, from local honey to heirloom grains to...farm-fresh ice cream! She's thankful to all those who accompanied her on these culinary excursions—most notably to the young ones: Theo, Will, Alex, Ruby, and Olivia.

TABLE OF CONTENTS

Getting from Pasture to Market

Goats are cute, clever animals that have lived alongside humans for almost 11,000 years. And from the ancient Greek god Pan to the characters of "Three Billy Goats Gruff," they've long played roles in the stories we tell.

But what *exactly* do goats provide humans? When, where, why, and how did people first **domesticate** them? And why are they still used as **livestock** today?

Let's learn more about these **cloven** creatures with Gretta Winkelbauer, a farmer who harnesses their resources to make everything from candy to cheese.

[21ST CENTURY SKILLS LIBRARY]

Kids go together! Baby goats and humans make for natural companions.

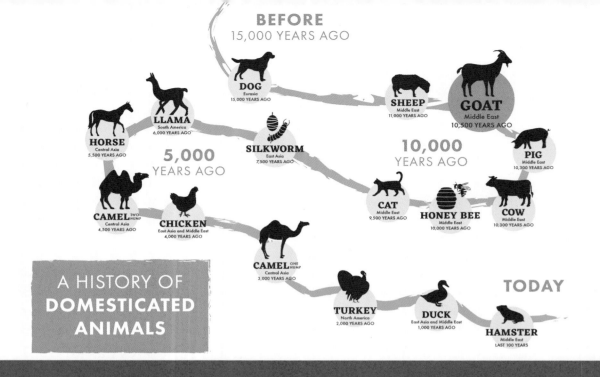

BEFORE
15,000 YEARS AGO

DOG
Eurasia
15,000 YEARS AGO

SHEEP
Middle East
11,000 YEARS AGO

GOAT
Middle East
10,500 YEARS AGO

LLAMA
South America
6,000 YEARS AGO

HORSE
Central Asia
5,500 YEARS AGO

5,000
YEARS AGO

SILKWORM
East Asia
7,500 YEARS AGO

10,000
YEARS AGO

PIG
Middle East
10,300 YEARS AGO

CAMEL TWO HUMP
Central Asia
4,500 YEARS AGO

CHICKEN
East Asia and Middle East
4,000 YEARS AGO

CAT
Middle East
9,500 YEARS AGO

HONEY BEE
Middle East
10,000 YEARS AGO

COW
Middle East
10,300 YEARS AGO

CAMEL ONE HUMP
Central Asia
3,000 YEARS AGO

A HISTORY OF
**DOMESTICATED
ANIMALS**

TURKEY
North America
2,000 YEARS AGO

DUCK
East Asia and Middle East
1,000 YEARS AGO

TODAY

HAMSTER
Middle East
LAST 100 YEARS

It is believed that dogs were the first domesticated animals.

Humans and goats began their shared journey in the ancient Middle East. At first, **hunter-gatherers** there pursued wild goats for meat. Over a long period of time, these **nomadic** groups started to herd them. As people began to live closer to goats, they realized that the animals could also provide milk and fibers. These two resources could be used for both food and clothing, two critical human needs.

As roving bands of ancient humans moved from place to place and populated the globe, they brought the agile and easygoing goat along with them. Today, goats are the most geographically widespread livestock species on our planet.

European colonists brought domesticated goats to the Americas as early as the 1400s. Christopher Columbus and his crew made their voyages with goats, pigs, sheep, horses, and cows. More than 500 years later, the United States has an estimated 2.6 million goats.

Let's travel to a 25-acre (10 hectares) farm in Pecatonica, Illinois, to meet 52 of these goats. Here, farmer Gretta follows in the footsteps of our ancestors, using goats' milk to make soap, cheese, lip balm, and more.

Gretta and her husband Eric share their 25-acre (10-hectare) farm with more than 50 goats.

Presidential Goats

While dogs and cats may be the most common presidential pets, other animals—including goats—have roamed the halls of the White House. In the 1860s, the Lincolns shared the home with a pair of goats named Nanny and Nanko. Like most goats, Nanny and Nanko were grazers and enjoyed munching on everything from the White House lawn to flower bulbs and furniture.

The Lincolns' sons, Tad and Willie, sometimes surprised guests by racing through the White House in goat-pulled carts. "Honest Abe" himself was also known to enjoy the goats' company. Mrs. Lincoln's seamstress, Elizabeth Keckley, remembered him declaring, "I believe they are the kindest and best goats in the world."

While the Lincolns' goats were the first **ruminants** to live in the White House, they weren't the last. Benjamin Harrison also had a goat named Old Whiskers. But as legend has it, Harrison's goat was not nearly as friendly.

The Road to Goat Farming

Gretta is not a newcomer to farming. She grew up on a farm in Michigan surrounded by animals. Her family's **farmstead** was home to cats, chickens, rabbits, sheep, and up to 50 sled dogs! Gretta and her dad were **mushers** and raised huskies.

Gretta also had one goat named Sundance. Even as a child, she was charmed by these creatures. "They have so much personality!" she says. "They're just fun animals."

She dreamed of making goats a part of her life as an adult, but a busy schedule as a teacher in Chicago made that next to impossible.

Gretta's love of animals and the outdoors began at a young age, and was encouraged by her parents.

Goats were the first animals to be used for milk by humans.

But next to impossible *isn't* impossible. Gretta was determined to have her goats and milk them too! Where could she learn about farming as a career? How could she combine her *want* of working with goats with her *need* to earn a living?

Gretta looked for places where she could practice the art and science of farming. In 2011, she was accepted into a farm business development program at Prairie Crossing Farms in Grayslake, Illinois. She spent 4 years in the program.

[21ST CENTURY SKILLS LIBRARY]

Gretta went to school to learn the business of raising goats.

etta's goats

Coconut, Sustainable Palm
and Organic Sweet Orange
Essential Oil

Net wt.   ounces

grettasgoats.com
498 N Farwell Bridge Rd
Pecatonica IL 60030

Gretta's handmade soaps put her business on the map.

At the time Gretta started at Prairie Crossing, she had three goats that pastured about a mile (1.6 kilometers) away from her home. Every day, she would travel to this farm to care for and hand-milk the goats. She took their milk home to her kitchen to make soap. This soap was the key to launching her new career as a full-time goat farmer.

She was already selling her handmade soaps at local markets and online. This **direct-to-consumer** model required almost no **marketing** and allowed her to meet customer needs.

Then, things changed.

Gretta's products were featured on Oprah.com's list of "Perfect Presents." After this **publicity**, she and her three goats struggled to meet surging demand. Her kitchen-turned-soap-making-workshop was getting *very* cramped.

It was time for Gretta and her husband to find a place where the herd and the business could expand.

What It Takes

One **natural resource** that all farmers need is land—whether they work on a small or large scale, raise livestock, or harvest grains and vegetables. This need is what brought Gretta and Eric to Pecatonica.

The couple's decision to move was based on their interest in having a certified dairy. They didn't just want to keep making soap. They wanted to start making cheese. To do this, they needed to invest in additional natural resources: land and more goats. As the farm grew, they also had to grow their **human capital**. So they hired additional staff to help with milking, soap making, and farmers' markets.

Gretta and Eric's farm in Pecatonica provides the space needed for their goats and other livestock, like these free-range chickens.

Farming is a full-time, year-round job. The spring kidding season marks one of the busiest times of year.

Gretta and Eric's interest in having a certified dairy also meant investing in **physical capital**. Because of the small staff and growing herd, they use milking machines. To ensure the safety of this milk supply, they take it to an offsite laboratory to test for bacteria.

Farm life is seasonal.

Spring is very busy, bringing new kids—or baby goats—to the farm.

During warm months, goats graze **rotationally**. Gretta uses her pickup truck and portable fencing to move the pasture every two days. A flock of chickens follows the herd, scratching through the manure and pushing it into the ground. This fertilizes the soil. These seasons are also the time of year when milk production is highest.

In the winter, the goats' milk dries up. The animals rest and eat hay in the barn, often snuggling together in big heaps to keep warm.

But winter doesn't mean downtime for Gretta. Anticipating the quiet, she freezes milk from the peak of the season. This

GRETTA'S GOATS
GRADE A MEDIUM EGGS

198 N FARWELL BRDIGE ROAD
PECATONICA, IL 61063
WWW.GRETTASGOATS.COM

PACK DATE: 117
SELL BY: 25-may

CE# 11938
REFRIGERATED AT OR BELOW 15°F

SAFE HANDLING INSTRUCTIONS: to prevent illness from bacteria: keep eggs refrigerated, cook eggs until yolks are firm, and cook foods containing eggs thoroughly.

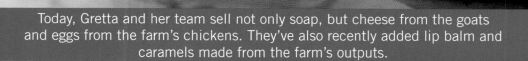

Today, Gretta and her team sell not only soap, but cheese from the goats and eggs from the farm's chickens. They've also recently added lip balm and caramels made from the farm's outputs.

allows her to keep making soap during the coldest and darkest months of the year. She and her staff continue to feed and care for all the animals on the farm.

A World of Resources

Gretta is an agricultural **entrepreneur**, which means she coordinates the resources (or **inputs**) below to make products (or **outputs**).

Natural Resources—Land and Animals: Natural resources are just what they sound like: materials that come directly from nature. These resources exist without human intervention. Some natural resources, like sun and wind, are **renewable**. Others, like oil and coal, are **nonrenewable**. What natural resources does Gretta's business need to succeed?

Human Resources—Labor: Human resources are the "people" aspect of any operation. In Gretta's case, it's the knowledge, skills, experience, and abilities that she needs to run her business. It also includes any help that she need from other employees.

Physical Resources—Capital: Physical resources are the things that you need to help operate a business, like machines, computers, and buildings. What physical resources does the farm need?

Getting to Market

Gretta notes that running a farm comes with challenges. The work is 24 hours a day, 7 days a week. Farmers don't get regular vacations, as they cannot afford to be away from their land and animals for long periods of time. For Gretta, this means she misses out on some key things, like family events and holidays.

Land—particularly near a city like Chicago—can be expensive. Gretta and Eric made a major life change by moving to the small **rural** community of Pecatonica, where this natural resource was more affordable. While the move allowed them to have the farm and business they wanted, it

Gretta and Tim often miss out on holiday festivities to take care of their goats.

Gretta's Goats exists in the real world *and* online.

also meant being farther away from their network of family and friends. This is another major sacrifice that came with owning and operating their farm.

Early on in the business, Gretta had the good fortune of getting publicity from Oprah.com and from companies like Crate & Barrel. This helped bring her products to a wide range of consumers around the world.

Today, she continues to connect with new and existing customers in a variety of ways. During farmers' market season, Gretta and Eric make weekly journeys to Chicago. There they sell cheese and soap—along with new offerings like lip balm, goats' milk caramels, and eggs from the chickens—at Logan Square Farmers' Market. Their products can also be found in local shops.

The farm has a virtual footprint too, with an Etsy shop and a strong social media presence. Gretta manages the farm's Instagram and Facebook pages, which are used to promote happenings like goat yoga and cheese-making classes. These fun and social events continue to draw new people to the farm.

Gretta and Eric look forward to expanding their farm to include therapy programs.

What's next for Gretta and her goats?

Before Gretta began farming, she was a Braille teacher who worked with blind children. She also trained seeing-eye and service dogs.

Moving forward, Gretta would like to combine her experience as an educator with her current work as a farmer. "I know that being outside in nature and being with animals was hugely therapeutic for my students," she explains. She and Eric hope to offer that experience to more and more kids as the farm continues to grow.

Gretta knows that the bond between people and goats can be powerful.

Assistance and Therapy Animals

Lots of animals are used for assistance and as therapy. They fulfill many functions, from retrieving items for their human partners to providing support for those facing mental health issues.

While goats aren't as commonly seen in these roles as dogs, cats, or even horses, that will likely change with time. Gretta predicts that their affectionate nature will lead people to start considering them for this important work.

Taking Informed Action

Market Day!

Are you interested in learning more about being a farmer? Do you want to know more about where your food comes from and how it's produced? If so, Gretta recommends that you talk to farmers and food producers! Encourage your teacher to invite a farmer to your class. Visit your local farmers' market and talk to the people who make your food.

Don't know where to begin the conversation? Remember that *who, what, when, where, why,* and *how* are the core questions for starting any discussion.

Need some examples? Here are a few questions that we put to Gretta:

- How did you get interested in farming?
- Who helped you learn about farming? When and where did you start?
- What resources do you need to operate the farm?
- Why do you think it's important for people to buy local products?
- What are the most challenging things about running your farm and business?
- What's the best thing about farming?

So grab your notebook and a pen and get to the farmers' market! There's a friendly maker just waiting to field your questions.

GLOSSARY

cloven (KLOH-ven) split in two, as in a goat's hooves

direct-to-consumer (duh-REKT TOO kuhn-SOO-mur) selling a product directly to a buyer, as opposed to a store, which may resell it

domesticate (duh-MES-tih-kate) to tame (an animal) so it can be used by people

entrepreneur (ahn-truh-pruh-NUR) a person who coordinates resources (natural resources, human capital, physical capital) to create a product and make a profit

farmstead (FARM-sted) a farm and the buildings around it

human capital (HYOO-muhn KAP-ih-tuhl) a person's knowledge and experience that can be used in operating a business

hunter-gatherers (HUHN-tur GATH-ur-urz) nomadic people who lived mainly by hunting, gathering, and fishing

inputs (IN-puts) factors needed to make a product, such as natural resources, human capital, and physical capital

livestock (LIVE-stahk) farm animals

marketing (MAHR-kit-ing) promoting and advertising a business or service

mushers (MUSH-urz) competitive sled dog racers

natural resource (NACH-ur-uhl REE-sors) material like land or water that occurs in nature that can be used for economic gain

nomadic (NOH-mad-ik) not settled, migrant, wandering from place to place

nonrenewable (nahn-rih-NOO-uh-buhl) natural resources that can run out, such as oil and coal

outputs (OUT-puts) the amount of goods produced using various inputs in a given period of time

physical capital (FIZ-ih-kuhl KAP-ih-tuhl) resources like machines and equipment that people need to run a business

publicity (puh-BLIS-ih-tee) attention to a person, good, or service, often through a media outlet

renewable (rih-NOO-uh-buhl) natural resources that never run out, like the sun and wind

rotationally (roh-TAY-shuh-nuhl-ee) moved (pasture animals) to different, fenced forage areas to help manage and conserve land

ruminants (ROO-mih-nuhnts) types of mammals with multiple stomachs, such as cows, sheep, antelopes, deer, giraffes, and goats

rural (ROOR-uhl) in the country

FURTHER READING

Banyard, Antonia, and Paula Ayer. *Eat Up! An Infographic Exploration of Food.* Toronto: Annick Press, 2017.

Kenney, Karen Latchana. *Pygmy Goat.* Vero Beach, FL: Rourke Educational Media, 2016.

Mickelson, Trina. *Free-Range Farming.* Minneapolis: Lerner Publications, 2016.

Reeves, Diane Lindsey. *Food & Natural Resources: Exploring Career Pathways.* Ann Arbor, MI: Cherry Lake Publishing, 2017.

Vogel, Julia. *Save the Planet: Local Farms and Sustainable Foods.* Ann Arbor, MI: Cherry Lake Publishing, 2010.

INDEX